A Pony Called Magic

You'll wish you had a pony like

Magic!

D0513120

A Pony Called Magic

You'll wish you had a pony like Magic!

A Pony Called Magic
Bumper Collection

Sheryn Dee

Illustrated by Matt Cosgrove

HAPPY CAT BOOKS

For my beautiful fairy god-daughter, Jessie.
And to celebrate the memories of Nor West Bend station.
S.D.

The illustrator wishes to thank Charlotte and her pony
Joey for all their help.   M.C.

Published by
Happy Cat Books
An imprint of Catnip Publishing Ltd
14 Greville Street
London
EC1N 8SB

First published in 2003 by the Australian Broadcasting Corporation, GPO
Box 994 Sydney, NSW 2001

This edition first published 2007
1 3 5 7 9 10 8 6 4 2

A CIP catalogue record for this book is available from the British Library

ISBN   978-1-905117-74-1

Printed in Poland

www.catnippublishing.co.uk

Contents

Magic and the Best Day

The night sky twinkled with a million stars and a soft breeze tickled the treetops. Everyone at Big Bend Station lay asleep in their beds, dreaming of their favourite things. Jessie Brock was sleeping soundly under her snug quilt. It was tucked up around her shoulders and she was as warm as toast. Pictures of black stallions, brown geldings, bay mares and newborn foals all watched over her as she slept.

As dawn crept across the countryside, Jessie opened her eyes just a tiny bit. It was almost light. All of a sudden she remembered something. This was no ordinary morning. This was her birthday — her seventh birthday! Jessie's heart beat faster and her skin tingled.

All the horses on the walls seemed to be looking at Jessie and grinning, wishing her a happy birthday. Jessie slipped out of bed and tiptoed out of her room. Her parents' bedroom was very quiet. They were still fast asleep.

Jessie decided not to wake them up yet, so she stretched and yawned her way into the lounge. She pulled back the curtain to see if her dog Max was asleep on the verandah. But instead of Max, she saw something quite unbelievable.

A pony was standing outside the window, looking straight inside at her.

Jessie ran back into her parents' bedroom and shook her mum gently. 'Mum, Mum … wake up! It's important.' Jessie's mum opened her eyes. 'Mum, there's a … a pony outside the window! Truly really! An actual pony! Come quick!' said Jessie.

Mum squinted at her with sleepy eyes. 'A pony? What kind of pony, Jessie?'

'A real pony! With a black mane,' Jessie exclaimed.

Jessie's dad woke up and grunted, 'A pony? Outside the window? Impossible! You're dreaming, Jess. All our horses are in the stables. And we don't have any ponies!' He turned over to go back to sleep.

Mum yawned and rubbed her eyes. Then she gently prodded Dad. 'Come on, we'd better have a look.'

Jessie took her sleepy parents by the hands and led them to the window. Jessie's hands were trembling ... she almost expected the pony to be gone. Then, no-one would believe she had ever seen anything. But the pony was there, just as before.

'See?' she whispered, gazing at the most perfect pony she'd ever seen. 'He's beautiful. And he's real!'

'Wow!' exclaimed Dad. 'He's a beauty.'

'Mmmm,' said Mum. 'Curious too. See how he's looking at you, Jessie.'

'He's magic!' squeaked Jessie. Her heart was skipping with excitement. 'He can't be real ... but he is!'

Mum and Dad weren't so sleepy anymore, and they had huge smiles on their faces. 'Happy Birthday, Jessie!' they said together.

Jessie threw her arms around them. 'You were tricking me, Dad,' she said. 'We do have a pony!'

Morning in the South Australian Riverland was glorious: the sun shone brightly, there were no clouds in the sky, and the fresh scent of the bush drifted on a gentle breeze. White cockatoos perched in rows high in the branches of the trees by the river, and skinks flitted around the leaves and twigs on the ground.

Jessie perched on the top rail of the horse paddock fence as her father showed her how to saddle up her new pony. Jessie admired his creamy buckskin coat, black mane and black tail. He was the most beautiful pony she'd ever seen. And he kept looking at Jessie. He seemed to know they were going to have lots of fun together.

While Dad brushed the pony down, Jessie jumped off the rail and unfolded the saddle blanket. Dad threw it over the pony's back, then carefully placed the saddle on top and gently buckled the girth. Next he fitted the bridle and showed Jessie how to smooth the mane around her pony's ears to make sure the bridle sat comfortably. Then Dad lifted the reins over the pony's head and, one at a time, stretched out each front leg. Dad knew a lot about horses because he had looked after them all his life.

'When you saddle up, always stretch out his front legs, Jessie,' explained Dad. 'Then the skin is free around the girth and doesn't get pinched.'

'Pinched!' exclaimed Jessie. 'No-one's going to pinch my pony!'

'That's right,' Dad chuckled, 'and the girth won't pinch your pony either, as long as you stretch out his front legs.'

'Can I ride him now, Dad?' Jessie was beginning to feel impatient.

'Soon enough, Jessie,' said Dad. 'Let's just check the hoofs for stones.'

'Okay,' Jessie agreed. 'How often do we have to do that, Dad?'

'Before and after every ride.'

Jessie pulled a face. It sounded like a lot of work.

'Well,' Dad winked, 'we have to look after our horses and ponies or they'll go lame and then we won't be able to ride them at all!'

Jessie nodded, trying very hard to be patient. She wanted to take good care of her pony. She stood back as Dad held up

each hoof and inspected it for tiny stones. She knew it wasn't safe to stand too close to a horse's back legs.

Suddenly Jessie thought of something. 'Dad, does my pony have a name?'

Dad shook his head slowly. 'No, we thought you would be able to find just the right name for him.'

'Well ...' began Jessie. 'How about Prince, or Lightning, or ...'

'There's no hurry, Jess,' said Dad. 'A name will come to you when it's good and ready.'

Jessie nodded. She hoped that Dad was right.

As Jessie and Dad finished saddling up, Mum came over with some sunscreen for Jessie's face.

'Do you know something, Mum?' said Jessie, as Mum rubbed in the cream. 'I wished for a pony on every wishbone I ever had.'

Mum smiled. 'Did you now? I never would have known!'

'Well I did,' said Jessie. 'And I wished for a pony on every stone I threw in Nan's wishing well. And now it's come true.'

Dad walked the pony over to the rail. Everything was now ready for Jessie's first ride.

'Here goes, Jess!' grinned Dad. 'Time to test drive this beast!'

Jessie felt her heartbeat quicken. She stroked her pony on the flank, lifted her left foot high into the stirrup and, all in one smooth movement, Dad hoisted her up onto the pony's back.

She wiggled her bottom into the saddle, slipped her right foot into the other stirrup and picked up the reins.

'How does he feel, Jess?' asked Dad.

'Great!' she replied. It was true. Right away she felt very safe, as though she really did belong on this pony's back. She could feel him flicking his black tail to swish away the flies. She leaned forwards to rub his neck and whisper in his ear. 'You are the best pony in the world. I love you.'

Dad stood in front of the pony and held his bridle. 'Just stand still for a minute, pat his neck and get used to each other. Then you can nudge him with your heels and walk him around,' suggested Dad.

Jessie did what Dad said. She rubbed her pony's neck and talked to him. After a while, she gently nudged him with her heels and they took their first steps together. They walked around slowly in a big circle and when Jessie stopped in front of her parents, she was grinning from head to toe.

'Still okay?' asked Mum.

'Oh, yes!' exclaimed Jessie. 'This pony and I fit together like magic.'

Dad nodded. He thought the two of them looked good together. 'Better get used to walking him for a while, Jess. Maybe try a trot later.'

'I know the rule Dad — walk in for a mile, walk out for a mile.'

Mum clapped her hands. 'You've got it, Jessie! That's how we warm the horses up and then settle them down.'

Jessie spent the next hour riding her new pony around the paddock while her parents watched. She had never felt so happy. She walked him round and round until she felt quite confident. Then, when Dad signalled it was time, she nudged the pony's flank again and he broke into a trot at once. When she pulled on the reins he stopped. Jessie felt very safe. She could tell that her pony liked having her on his back.

As they walked around the paddock together, Jessie chatted to her pony about the farm, and pointed everything out.

The wide old Murray River flowed along quietly at the far edge of the furthest paddock, glinting in the sun. Three pelicans flew by, heading towards the river to do some fishing, and high above them — way up in the sky — a wedge-tailed eagle circled lazily, searching the distant ground for some tasty morsel for lunch.

While they walked, her pony sniffed the fences and snorted as flies came too close to his nostrils. Now and then he flicked his black tail to let the flies know who was who. All of a sudden, just as Jessie was pointing out a flock of galahs, the pony spied a clump of green grass and stopped. He reached down to nibble the juicy leaves and pulled the reins from Jessie's hands.

'Hey!' Jessie complained. 'Stop that!' She reached forwards gently and collected the reins again, and her pony lifted his head. She nudged him with her heels and he walked on.

'Good on you!' called Dad from the fence. 'Keep him moving right along!'

At that moment Max raced out into the paddock, barking and chasing a bee.

Max was always chasing something. The pony stopped still again. He looked at Max suspiciously.

'It's just Max!' explained Jessie. 'Don't take any notice of him. He barks at everything — even butterflies!'

For a few seconds the pony watched Max closely. 'You'll get used to him,' coaxed Jessie. 'He's just a noisy dog!'

Jessie's pony seemed to understand and decided to ignore Max. He started to walk again and Jessie patted his sleek neck and shoulders happily.

'You really are special. I think you're magic,' she whispered. Suddenly Jessie knew what she wanted to call her pony. She sat up, kicked her heels and trotted back to the rail shouting, 'Mum! Dad!'

Her parents looked up in surprise.

'I've got it!' Jessie announced. 'I know his name!'

'Good!' said Mum. 'What is it?'

Jessie shifted her weight back in the saddle and said, 'Whoa.' The pony stopped at once, right beside Mum and Dad.

'See how he knows just what to do? Well, I think his name should be … Magic.'

Dad raised his eyebrows. 'What a name,' he said.

Mum ran her fingers through the thick black mane. 'Perfect,' she agreed. 'Magic is just right for this pony.'

Jessie had a lot to learn about looking after her pony. Mum and Dad had always looked after the horses on the property, but now Magic was Jessie's special responsibility.

First of all, Dad took off Magic's bridle, replaced it with a halter and tied the lead to the rail. Then he removed the saddle and saddle blanket from Magic's back. Jessie's first job was to brush her pony with a coarse scrubbing brush to remove the dust and loose hair. Because she was only seven and not very tall, Jessie had to stand on two bales of hay to reach Magic's back.

After brushing, Jessie squirted Magic down with a hose, and then she had to shampoo his creamy coat. She lathered him up with shampoo until her arms

looked just like sticks of frothy white fairy floss. Magic wasn't keen on all that shampoo, so Jessie squirted him down with the hose again.

The trickiest part was scraping all the water off Magic's back with a scraper. It was a bit like running a squeegee over the car windows. If Jessie's arms had been longer, it would have been a lot easier.

But she stretched around Magic's back as far as she could and Dad said that she was doing an excellent job. She scraped Magic's sides and his legs until hardly any water remained in his coat. When the scraping was finished, Jessie was completely covered in froth and water. Even her hair and ears were wet. Dad shook his head.

'Now I think I'll have to scrape you down, Jess!' he laughed.

'Have I finished yet, Dad?" asked Jessie, thinking about a hot bath.

'Not quite,' Dad grinned. 'Let's finish the job properly. I'll show you how to wash Magic's mane and tail.'

They filled a bucket with warm soapy water. At least it was warm water this time, and Jessie was happy to dip her arms in it. Then, while Dad held the bucket up to Magic's tail for a good soaking, Jessie used a shearing comb to drag out the knots. Luckily there weren't many knots and, by working on a little piece of tail at a time, Jessie was able to comb it out quickly.

Washing the mane was a different story. Jessie sat on Magic's back and, while Dad held the bucket steady, Jessie dipped the jet-black mane into the bucket and washed it bit by bit. Then she had to comb that out as well.

Before Jessie knew it, the whole afternoon had gone.

Dad and Jessie led Magic into his stall, filled up the water trough and gave him an alfalfa biscuit and a biscuit of hay and oats.

As Jessie sat on the top rail of the fence around the stables, dangling her legs and watching her freshly washed, gleaming new pony eat his dinner, the sun began to set over the riverland station. The sky was pale pink, and the horizon was orange and purple. All kinds of birds flew overhead on their way to and from the river. Insects flitted around the leafy bushes and an echidna waddled its lazy way across the paddock.

'There, Magic!' said Jessie happily. 'This is your new home. Isn't it beautiful?'

Jessie breathed deeply and sighed a long, happy sigh. This was the best day of her life. There was only one way to describe it — a dream come true.

A Big
Day Out

It was spring at Big Bend Station. The morning sun lit up the bush with a fresh, clear sparkle and the scent of a thousand new leaves and flowers filled the air. Jessie bounced up and down on her bed with joy. It was Saturday today, so she and Magic could spend the whole day together. She would take him a carrot and an apple as a treat; she had already packed them in the purple backpack Nan had given her for her birthday. A purple water bottle and purple notepad were also in the backpack.

Jessie put on her riding clothes and her new purple socks. 'Nan must really love purple!' she thought.

Jessie burst into the kitchen ready to eat breakfast quickly. Mum was drinking tea and reading the paper. She had

already been out to feed the horses so she was having a quiet moment to herself.

'Morning, Jessie,' Mum smiled. 'You look ready for action.'

'I am!' Jessie replied as she gave Mum a hug. 'Magic action. We're going to have heaps of fun today.'

'Good!' Mum was happy that Jessie loved her new pony so much. 'Dad and I will be working around the house so we can keep an eye on you.'

'OK,' said Jessie. 'Magic and I will check out the farm. Magic still has a lot to learn about his new home.'

'How about some breakfast first?' said Mum.

After breakfast Jessie grabbed her riding hat and kissed Mum goodbye. 'See you later, alligator!' she said.

'In a while, crocodile,' replied Mum, with a smile.

Jessie skipped out of the back door and up the track towards the stables. She came around the corner of the shed and there was Magic, beautiful as ever with his creamy coat and black mane. He flicked his long, glossy tail when he saw Jessie in her boots and riding hat. He was eager to get going too.

Jessie found Dad working around the stables.

'Hi, Dad, I'm ready!'

'OK, Jess. If you give me a hand with this bale of hay, I'll help you saddle up.'

Jessie wanted to ride Magic right away, but there were always important jobs to be done on a farm. She grabbed the other end of the hay bale and helped Dad hoist it onto the pick-up. As it landed, Dad and Jessie let out a big sigh of relief together.

'That was heavy,' gasped Jessie.

'Sure was!' Dad agreed. 'That's the thing about farm animals — their dinner always weighs a ton!'

Jessie shifted impatiently from one foot to the other.

'OK, Jess,' said Dad. 'I've got the message loud and clear. Let's saddle up.'

Dad helped to get Magic ready for a big day out. His creamy coat gleamed from brushing and his big dark eyes twinkled. Magic seemed to know it was time for some fun.

At last Dad boosted Jessie into the saddle. She was too small to mount Magic on her own from the ground.

At first Jessie walked Magic around the whole paddock to warm him up. Then she nudged him gently with her heels and Magic broke into a trot. Jessie concentrated on her technique, trying to get the rise and fall just right. After a while she nudged Magic again and they began to canter. This was Jessie's favourite kind of riding! She loved the feel of the wind in her face as they cantered down the paddock.

Dad watched from the stables. Now and then he would call out a few hints to help Jessie ride better. Jessie listened carefully — she wanted to be the best rider ever and her dad knew everything about horses and riding.

Dad had to get back to work, so he gave Jessie a wave. He knew she was happy riding around the paddock on her own, practising her new skills.

Jessie and Magic went round and round the paddock. Sometimes they walked, sometimes they trotted, and sometimes they cantered. Sometimes Jessie felt really good and at other times she felt a bit wobbly. When she felt wobbly, she slowed Magic down to a walk, chatted to him for a while and started again.

Jessie practised turning Magic around before they reached the fence. Soon she was able to guide him wherever she wanted him to go. Jessie felt very proud of herself and Magic.

As they rode along near the fence, Jessie noticed that the gate was open. Someone must have left it unlatched. She tried to close it by reaching down from Magic's back but it was too difficult and Magic didn't like it. He pulled on the reins and tossed his head.

Then Jessie had an idea. 'Magic,' she whispered in a quiet voice. 'Do you feel like an adventure?'

Magic flicked his glossy black tail.

'Right!' Jessie announced. 'We're going to see a little bit of the farm.'

She guided Magic through the gate and walked carefully along the track. She felt a bit naughty — she hadn't asked Dad if she could ride outside the paddock. But Magic was a perfect pony and Jessie felt very safe. She sat up straight and gently nudged his flanks with her heels.

They followed Jessie's favourite walking trail through the trees. 'This is good for you, Magic,' she said. 'You'll never get to know the farm if we stay in a paddock all the time!'

The farm was alive with birds in the trees and butterflies fluttering around the flowers. There were diggings in the ground where echidnas had been.

'I bet you've never seen an echidna, Magic,' said Jessie. 'They have spines to protect them, and their babies are called puggles!'

Magic snorted as a flock of screeching white cockatoos suddenly flew up from the flood plain. They rose like a swirling white cloud and the noise was deafening. Magic snorted and stepped sideways, and Jessie nearly slipped off his back.

'Magic!' she cried. 'It's all right. They're only birds. They always make that screeching noise.'

Magic wasn't sure. He tossed and turned his head and Jessie had a hard time keeping hold of the reins. But finally she calmed him, and they stood quietly together until all the birds had flown away.

Jessie patted Magic's neck. It was hot and damp. She knew that the birds had made him nervous. 'You'll have to get used to this, Magic. This is your home.' She nudged him into a walk. 'Come on, just a little bit further and then we'll go home.'

Magic settled down and soon they were trotting happily along the track. Just as they came to the top of a gentle hill, Jessie saw a big sleepy lizard sunning itself in the middle of the track. She slowed her pony down. After his scare with the birds, Jessie wasn't sure how Magic would react to this creature. She brought him to a halt, slipped her feet out of the stirrups and slid down off his back.

Then she looped the reins over her arm and led Magic to get a better look at the sleepy lizard. She crept up very close and admired its scaly skin.

The lizard scurried across the sand.

'Come on, Magic,' Jessie whispered, 'let's follow it.'

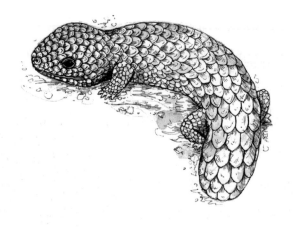

Jessie let go of the reins and quietly followed the sleepy lizard between the tussocks of grass and fallen twigs. Jessie was amazed at how fast it could run when it wanted to.

'It's all right, Sleepy, I'm not going to hurt you.'

She kept following the lizard until it disappeared under a big old log on the ground.

'Hey, Magic,' Jessie called out. 'See where Sleepy lives?'

Jessie turned to see what Magic thought of all this. But Magic wasn't there. Jessie jumped up, tripped on a branch and fell backwards into a prickly bush.

'Ouch!' she squealed. As she tried to brush the prickles off her bottom, they stuck in her hands.

'Magic? Where are you?' Jessie's chest tingled and she felt a bit frightened. She hadn't heard Magic wander away.

She looked in every direction but there was no sign of Magic. Where could he be? This was his first time out in the bush and he could easily get lost.

Jessie slowly turned around in a big circle. Where was she? The bush looked the same in every direction. Jessie called out her pony's name.

'Magic! Where are you? You're not supposed to run away, you should be right here with me! Come back at once!'

Jessie began to run back to where she thought the track might be, but she was

so upset that she tripped over the same old prickly bush and landed flat on her face in the sand. Her hands tingled with the pain of the prickles.

'Ouch!' she cried again. 'I hate you, you mean old prickly bush!'

She sat up, her face streaked with dirt and sand and, right there, looking into her eyes, was her pony.

'Oh, Magic!' she cried, throwing her arms around his neck. 'Where have you been? I think we're lost!'

Tightly grasping the reins, Jessie looked around carefully. With Magic beside her again, it was suddenly easy to see the track. It was right there, just a couple of metres away, and Jessie breathed a big sigh of relief. They weren't lost after all.

Suddenly Jessie felt very thirsty and was glad that she'd brought her backpack. But before she could get to her water bottle, she had to carefully pick the prickles from her hands. At last Jessie was able to open the backpack and take a long swig of water from her purple bottle.

'That's better,' she sniffed. 'But I've had enough of this adventure, Magic. It's time to go home. But I can't get on your back alone. You'll have to help me.'

Jessie led Magic over to a big old log, and climbed onto it.

'Come on, Magic, stand still.' But Magic didn't want to stand still beside the log, and Jessie grew impatient.

'Magic! I said stand still.'

Magic moved his hoofs on the soft sand. This was new to him. He decided to shuffle around, eating big clumps of grass instead.

This gave Jessie an idea. Still balancing on the log, she reached inside her backpack and pulled out a big juicy carrot.

'Hey, Magic, look at this!' She held out the carrot.

Magic liked the look of it. He came closer and flashed his dark eyes at Jessie while she grabbed the reins.

Jessie let Magic take the carrot from her hand and, in one smooth motion, she put her left foot in the stirrup and swung her right leg over. Magic was happy to be chomping his carrot.

'Let's go,' said Jessie. She moved him into a gentle walk, perching carefully on the saddle (she could still feel the prickles in her bottom). She was hungry and wondered if it was lunchtime yet.

At last Jessie and Magic arrived back at the paddock. Dad was standing by the open gate, waiting.

'Hi, Dad!' Jessie called, relieved to see him.

Dad was frowning. 'Where have you been, Jessie? Mum and I have been worried about you. And you look the worse for wear.'

Jessie told Dad all about what had happened — the open gate, the sleepy lizard, losing Magic, the prickles, everything!

Dad scratched his head. 'Well, Jessie, you should have told us where you'd gone. I was about to come looking for you.'

Jessie slipped off her pony and put her arms around Dad. 'I know!' she said, giving him a big hug. 'I'm really sorry. I was a bit frightened really. And I did miss you.'

'OK,' said Dad. 'You'd better go and look after Magic. And when you're all cleaned up, we'll have a chat and sort out some rules.'

Later that afternoon, Jessie sat on the fence and fed Magic some apples. She thought about the rules her parents had discussed with her: staying inside the paddock unless Mum or Dad said she could go further; making sure someone always knew where she was; not trying any fancy riding without her parents around, and a few more as well. Mum had written the rules in the purple notepad so Jessie wouldn't forget them.

Jessie decided the rules were all good rules. It wasn't much fun feeling frightened, or losing your pony, or being covered in prickles!

For now, Magic seemed happy to stay close to Jessie and eat his treats. They'd had their first real adventure together today and Jessie would never forget it.

Riding Out After the Storm

When a great storm rolls into the South Australian Riverland, gusty winds whip up the Murray River. Twigs and leaves fly off tall gum trees, swirling in a jumble on the ground, and animals shelter cosily inside their homes. Sometimes big branches come crashing down, making new homes for ground animals. Old trees sometimes topple over to make way for young saplings.

One night, Jessie woke up to the sound of wind whistling around the house. Her bedroom window rattled and rain pounded onto the iron roof above her. Suddenly she felt a movement at the end of her bed and she sat up. Max the dog jumped into her arms and licked her face.

'Yuck, Max!' Jessie said. 'You can sleep on my bed but don't lick my face!'

Jessie slipped out of bed and drew back the curtain. Raindrops ran down the window and the dark branches of a gum tree waved in the distance.

Jessie climbed back into bed again and Max snuggled beside her. The storm raged outside but Jessie felt safe under her quilt. Mum and Dad always said that rain was like liquid gold. The more it rained the happier they were.

Jessie loved the rain too. It was just the wind she didn't like so much. She pulled the quilt over her ears so the rattling window wasn't so loud.

When Jessie woke up the next morning, the wind had stopped and all the rain had made the earth smell fresh. The trees and bushes were sparkling clean with the dust washed off their leaves. Even the air smelled brand new.

Jessie stretched, then dressed in her riding gear: long trousers, a long-sleeved shirt, hat and boots. This would be a great day for a ride on her pony, Magic.

'Hi, Jessie,' smiled Mum as Jessie hopped up on the kitchen stool to eat breakfast. A glass of orange juice and a big bowl of cereal were waiting for her. Mum was already working on the computer, sorting out business matters. Because she was looking forward to riding Magic, Jessie ate her breakfast very quickly. Then she hopped down and gave her Mum a big hug.

'Thanks for brekkie, Mum — I'm going to use up lots of energy riding my pony today!'

'Did you hear the storm in the night, Jessie?' asked Mum. 'There will be lots of branches down — maybe even whole trees, so be careful where you ride.'

Jessie finished the last of her juice and nodded.

'I'll be extra careful, Mum, promise.'

'Off you go then, and have fun.' Mum smiled at Jessie.

Jessie's eyes twinkled. 'We will!'

Dad was in the stables, brushing down his beautiful bay mare, Jezebel. Magic was nearby, snuffling about in a bag of oats.

'Hi, Dad,' greeted Jessie. 'Hello, Magic, my amazing pony!'

Magic had been a present for Jessie's seventh birthday. She remembered that day perfectly — it had been the most exciting day of her life! When she had pulled back the curtain in the lounge to look for Max, a beautiful buckskin pony had stared back at her through the window. It had been a dream come true.

Dad looked at Jessie. 'Well, Jess, I guess you're in a riding mood today, all dressed up in that riding gear!'

Jessie put her hands on her hips and gave her Dad a mischievous look.

'You got it, Dad! Would you please help me saddle up?'

'Sure. I've finished grooming Jezebel anyway. And it's about time Magic took his nose out of that empty bag of oats.'

Dad helped Jessie saddle up. Together they threw the saddle rug over Magic's back, then Dad lifted Jessie's leather saddle off the hook and buckled it neatly around the pony's girth. They stretched out Magic's front legs, checked his hoofs for stones, checked the stirrups and adjusted the reigns.

Jessie had become such a good rider that Dad sometimes gave her and Magic jobs to do around the farm. And after a storm, there were always lots of things to be done.

'So what do you think, Dad? Any jobs for us today?' asked Jessie.

Dad looked thoughtful for a minute. 'Tell you what, Jess. Why don't you and Magic check the fences?'

Jessie grinned. That was a good job. Sometimes a branch would land on a fence and crush it and the sheep would get out, or the cattle from next door would walk right in. Jessie's job was to report back to Dad where the fences were broken.

'Sure, Dad. Magic and I can do that, easy!' said Jessie.

'Great,' said Dad. 'Just check the fences in this paddock and the next one. I'll do the top paddocks later.'

Jessie and Magic set off happily. The fences were easy to follow, but it was important to walk alongside them carefully because after a storm there could be unexpected obstacles lying across the track.

'What a mess this storm has made, Magic!' exclaimed Jessie. Branches and twigs were lying everywhere. Jessie looked up into the high branches of the trees by the river.

'I wonder if the birds are all right. I bet some of them have lost their nests. They'll have to build new ones. And what about their poor little chicks?'

But all the birds seemed their usual selves. In fact, they were busier and noisier than ever. Pelicans glided across the river, a blue and white kingfisher sat on a low branch over the water waiting for a special fish for his lunch, and honeyeaters darted busily about the flowers, drinking the delicious nectar.

Jessie turned to ride along the next fence, when suddenly she spied something. There was a bird's nest lying on the ground — just in front of Magic's hoof!

'WHOA!' shouted Jessie as she shifted her weight back in the saddle. Magic

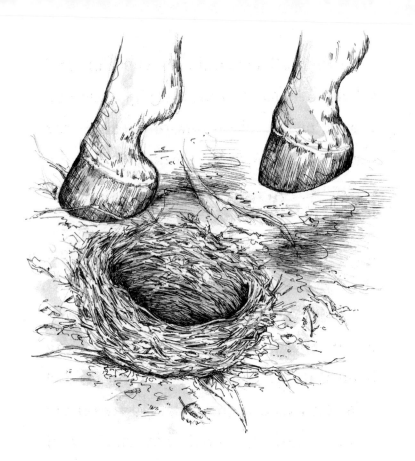

stopped immediately. Jessie leaned
forwards to look at the nest. There were
a few twigs and feathers scattered about,
but there was nothing in the nest. But
then, out of the corner of her eye, Jessie
saw a tiny movement beneath a twig.

At first, all she could see was fluff and a beak. It was the tiniest thing Jessie had ever seen. Looking more closely, she could just make out a head, eyes, little feet and a body that seemed to be half fluff and half skin.

Jessie was spellbound. Even Magic stood completely still.

Jessie knew straight away what she had to do. She carefully turned Magic away from the bird and the nest, and guided him towards a big old log resting on the ground. She stroked his neck and whispered in his ear. 'Now listen, Magic. You have to help me by not fidgeting. I'm going to slide off and I want you to keep still, okay?'

Jessie slipped her feet out of the stirrups and eased her right leg over

Magic's back. Then she slid easily to the ground, gathered the reins and tied them to the log.

She raised her finger to her lips and looked Magic in the eye, 'Shhhhh. Don't move, Magic.'

Jessie tiptoed over to the baby bird on the ground. She knelt down for a closer look. The bird looked up at her with its tiny brown eyes and made the faintest cheeping sound.

'Where are your mother and father?' Jessie asked softly. 'Don't they know where you are?' She looked up into the big trees and scanned the branches, but couldn't see any sign of its parents. 'Well you can't stay here,' she added. 'It's not safe. Do you want to come home with us?'

The baby bird fluttered its downy feathers as Jessie reached out to pick it up. But then Jessie paused. What could she carry it in? The only thing she could see was the broken nest. Then she had a great idea. She could carry the bird inside the nest, and tuck the nest inside her riding hat. Brilliant!

Jessie unfastened her hat and slipped it off her head. She scooped up the nest and packed it snugly inside the hat. 'Look, Magic. It's perfect!' she said. Magic snorted and flicked his long black tail.

Jessie carefully gathered up the baby bird and cupped it in her hands. She could feel its tiny, trembling body. Jessie knew she had found it just in time. She laid it gently in the nest and soothingly stroked its fluff.

'It's all right, you're safe now. You're coming home with us.'

Then Jessie realised that she couldn't ride Magic back to the house without wearing her riding hat. Mum and Dad had said she must never ride without her hat because it was too dangerous.

Jessie looked at the baby bird and shook her head. 'Guess what?' she sighed. 'We'll have to walk all the way home. And Magic, you'll just have to follow us.'

Jessie looped her arm through Magic's reins and set off home along the track. She carried the riding hat, with nest and baby bird inside, as carefully as she could. The tiny bundle of fluff didn't seem to be moving much anymore, but its beak opened now and then. Jessie hoped that Mum and Dad would know what to do.

They walked as quickly as Jessie could manage. Occasionally, Magic stopped to chew on a clump of grass, but then Jessie gave him a gentle tug on the reins to remind him that they were in the middle of a very important job — even more important than checking the fences!

It was a calm, cloudy day and the bush was quietly recovering from last night's storm. Even the leaves on the trees

and shrubs were still. Perhaps the bush was watching her, Jessie thought. Perhaps it was hoping that she could save the baby bird.

Jessie and Magic seemed to walk for ages along the sandy track by the fence. Jessie tried to hurry but her little legs were tired and her arms ached from carrying the riding hat steady for so long.

When they passed the big tree at the corner of the paddock, Jessie saw a cloud of dust. Then she heard the galloping hoofs of her father's horse, Jezebel, coming towards them.

'Dad!' called Jessie.

'Jessie!' he exclaimed, as he pulled up alongside her. 'What's wrong? Why are you walking?'

'Look,' said Jessie, holding up her hat to show him the baby bird in the nest.

Dad looked worried. 'Come on,' he said. 'Up behind me.' With his strong arms he reached down and pulled Jessie up behind him on the saddle. 'Don't worry about Magic,' he reassured her. 'He'll follow us home.'

Dad rode Jezebel back to the house. Jessie cradled the riding hat under one arm and held on tightly to her father's waist with the other arm. As soon as they arrived at the house he jumped off, grabbed Jessie and the hat, and they hurried inside.

Mum took one look at the tiny creature that was barely breathing and knew exactly what to do. Within a minute she had some special mixture in a small plastic dropper, like the ones doctors use, and was holding it to the fragile beak. Jessie held her breath, waiting to see what would happen. At first the bird didn't respond, but when a few drops went down its throat, the tiny creature started to cheep for more.

'Oh, look, it's alive!' said Jessie.

'And hungry too,' added Mum. She fed the tiny bird a few more drops of the precious mixture.

Dad carefully tucked the nest into a shoebox and Mum fitted a hot towel around the nest to keep it warm.

'Jessie,' said Dad, as he handed back her riding hat, 'you have done a very brave and wonderful thing. You have saved this little bird just in time.'

'Do you think it will be all right?' asked Jessie.

'I hope so, Jessie,' said Mum, making sure the baby bird was cosy. 'Thanks to you, I think it'll be just fine.'

Dad stood up and straightened his back. 'Right then, time to go and check the fences. The job's not finished yet. Coming with me, Jess?'

Jessie and Dad spent the rest of the morning riding beside each other, checking the fences. In a couple of places branches had fallen across the wire, so Dad and Jessie had to lift the branches off

and fix the fences. They rode all around the farm, but there was no major storm damage. Dad was relieved.

When they returned to the stables, Dad and Jessie were ready for a rest.

'Thanks, Dad,' said Jessie. 'That was fun. And Magic loved it too.'

'Good,' replied Dad. "I reckon Magic is getting used to this place, don't you?'

Jessie smiled. 'He loves it here. I know he does.'

'Well,' said Dad, 'I'd love a cup of tea and a piece of cake, but I guess we'd better clean up these horses first.'

'Sure,' agreed Jessie. 'And then we can see how my tiny baby bird is going.'

'Of course,' Dad nodded. 'I wonder if it's grown into an eagle yet?'

Jessie gasped. 'An eagle? Is that what it is?'

Dad laughed. 'No, I was joking. An eagle builds a great big nest and your bird has a small nest. I don't know what kind of bird it is.'

Jessie looked pleased. 'Then it will be a surprise when it grows up. And,' she added, 'I don't care what kind of bird it is, I know what its name is going to be.'

Jessie was very tired after cleaning the horses but as soon as she reached the front door of the house, she dashed inside to see her baby bird. She was delighted to find the tiny ball of fluff looking stronger and cheepier than ever.

'You are very special,' whispered Jessie into the nest, 'and I'm going to call you Storm.'

As she drifted off to sleep that night, Jessie knew the wild storm of the night before had brought her another adventure with Magic. It had also brought her another Storm that she'd never forget.

Magic Helps Out

One morning, Jessie woke up to the sounds of shouting and running. She jumped out of bed, ran to the front door and looked out into the yard. Jessie couldn't believe her eyes and squealed with delight at the funny scene in front of her. It reminded her of a circus she had seen where clowns squirted water all over each other.

Mum and Dad were running about with tools and hoses, calling here, racing there, and all the time a great fountain of water was spurting out of a broken pipe. Max was barking madly and running in and out of the spray, getting drenched and then shaking all over Mum and Dad who were already soaking wet.

Jessie could see that help was needed, so she ran outside at full speed. At once,

water sprayed her in the eyes and she couldn't see a thing, so she turned and ran away again. Then she had a brainwave.

Jessie raced into the shed and grabbed a big bucket. She dragged it back into the yard and placed it cleverly to collect some of the water squirting out of the pipe. She was soon dripping wet but she was very pleased with herself.

Dad was grappling with the break in the pipe when all at once the waterspout died away to a trickle. Dad stood up to stretch his back.

'What happened, Dad?' called Jessie, still giggling. 'Why did the water stop?'

'Mum turned off the pump, so we can fix this thing!'

'But my bucket isn't full yet,'

complained Jessie. 'It was going to be a special drink for Magic, so we didn't waste the water.'

At that moment Mum reappeared.

'Jessie, you look like a drowned rat!' she laughed.

Jessie grinned. She was standing in a mud pool in pyjamas and bare feet. There was water everywhere, and in the middle of it all was Dad. He was covered in mud and hacking at the broken pipe with a saw.

Jessie had another brainwave. 'Hey, Dad, I think we should build a proper fountain in the front yard. It could spray water all day.'

Mum took Jessie by the hand and led her towards the laundry. 'I don't think Dad's in the mood for fountain talk right now,' she said.

Jessie and Mum took off their dripping pyjamas in the laundry and rubbed themselves dry with towels.

'I've had enough,' laughed Mum, towelling her wet hair. 'And it's only eight in the morning! I hope the baby likes a bit of excitement so early in the day.'

Jessie wiped the mud from her face and looked at Mum in a puzzled way. 'What baby?' she asked.

Mum took Jessie's hands and placed them on her tummy.

'This baby,' replied Mum. 'Our baby.'

Jessie was silent for a moment. Then she burst out, 'Are we having a baby, Mum?'

'Sure are,' nodded Mum. 'You're going to be a big sister.'

'Wow,' said Jessie. 'Dad!' she squealed as her father appeared at the laundry door. 'I'm going to have a little brother or sister ... did you know that? I can teach it how to ride Magic and how to check the fences and feed the horses and round up the sheep and collect the eggs and bath Max and ...'

'Steady on,' laughed Dad. 'This baby's got a bit of growing to do before any of that can happen!'

Jessie broke into a big smile. The baby was great news, and she gave Mum and Dad a big hug. She didn't even mind that Dad was still dripping water all over her.

'Come on, time to get cleaned up,' said Mum. 'I'm starving.'

After a hot shower, Dad made them all breakfast.

'Around here,' he said, buttering the toast, 'babies have to get used to lots of excitement, don't they, Jess?'

Jessie nodded. 'Sure do! There's always something going on,' she agreed.

'Trouble is,' said Dad, 'now I'm way

behind on my day's work. I have to move the sheep into the top paddock today, but before that I have to run into town for some plumbing supplies so I can fix the pipe.'

Jessie looked hopeful. 'Can I help too Dad?'

He shook his head. 'Not really, Jess. I have to go all over the farm today. And some of the jobs I really need to do on my own.'

Jessie shrugged. But she had already made up her mind to do something useful. She just had to figure out exactly what that would be.

While Dad was in town, Jessie sorted out all the clothes in her drawers. She pulled out everything that was too small for her and filled a big bag to give to the baby. Nan had made her a beautiful party dress with pink and gold ribbons threaded through the stitching. Although it was her favourite dress, Jessie had grown out of it now. 'Hmm,' she said to herself, before slipping it into the bag. 'If I have a baby brother I don't know if he'll want to wear this very often!'

When the bag of clothes was full, Jessie sorted out toys and filled another bag. There were teddies and a toy car that she didn't play with anymore, and a few picture books.

But what could she do next? Mum was dozing in the bedroom and Jessie thought

it best not to bother her, especially with a baby inside her tummy that had some growing to do.

What Jessie really wanted was to ride her pony, Magic. All of a sudden she knew exactly what to do. She pulled on her riding gear and boots, grabbed her riding hat and tiptoed out the front door.

Magic was waiting for her in his stable. He snorted and flicked his black mane and tail. Jessie lifted the heavy saddle. Dad usually helped her get Magic ready but she knew how to do it. Luckily, Magic was very patient as Jessie buckled him up and stretched his legs. Jessie was sure Dad would be proud of her, saddling up all on her own, and she couldn't ask him for help anyway since he was so busy.

When everything was ready, Jessie led Magic to the fence rail. She climbed up and slipped easily into the saddle. It felt good to be on her pony again.

They walked and trotted around the paddock. Jessie could see the sheep in the next paddock standing around looking very bored.

'Poor sheep,' she said. 'They need something new to look at.'

And just then Jessie had yet another brilliant idea. It was a good day for great ideas, she thought. She could help Dad by moving the sheep for him! The sheep would be happy, her dad would be happy, and Jessie would have something really useful to do.

Jessie was excited. She hadn't moved the sheep by herself before, but she had helped heaps of times and it didn't seem too tricky. She made a plan.

Jessie rode Magic through the sheep paddock until she came to the gate. She would have to guide the sheep through this gate, then across the track and through the next gate into the top paddock. The sheep had done this a thousand times, so Jessie expected they'd know where to go.

First, Jessie had to open both gates. This meant she had to dismount from Magic, and then find a fence rail from which to mount him again. It was hard work already!

When the two gates were open, Jessie rode down around the sheep and began to round them up. Magic wasn't too keen on sheep and didn't want to get very close to them.

Jessie also had to teach him to turn sharply so they could stop the sheep moving in the wrong direction. Just when Jessie began to think it was all too difficult, the whole mob of sheep headed towards the first gate. She breathed a sigh of relief and took off after them. Magic thought it was fun now, and cantered back and forth happily, keeping the stragglers up with the mob.

At last the sheep crossed the track and reached the second gate, and through they went. Sheep always follow each other, and most of them wandered

through together into the top paddock. Jessie was feeling very pleased with herself.

There were only six sheep left in the bottom paddock now, and they were real slowcoaches. Jessie shouted at them to hurry up, and cantered up behind them. Suddenly they all took off through the gate. But the sheep in front turned down the track instead of going through the second gate and, of course, the other five sheep followed.

Jessie gasped. 'Silly sheep!' she yelled at them. 'Why did you do that? Can't you see where the others went?' Jessie groaned. 'What am I going to do now?'

The sheep inside the top paddock were grazing quietly on the grass already. Jessie slid out of the saddle and quickly shut the gate so they couldn't escape. Then she had to climb up onto the fence again to mount her pony. This was turning into really hard work, but Jessie couldn't give up now. She had a job to do!

The six runaway sheep had slowed down further along the track. Jessie walked Magic quietly along behind them, and tried to edge past them so they didn't scare. She hoped to be able to turn them around and head them back towards the gate. But one sheep decided to run and, of course, the others followed.

'Come back, silly sheep!' shouted Jessie.

The sheep kept running, with Jessie and Magic cantering behind, until they came to the open country. Now Jessie had a huge job to round these stragglers up and head them back up the track.

Jessie and Magic slowed to a walk again and Jessie looked around. She had never ridden Magic through this part of the farm. It was different. The trees were smaller and the ground was rockier. It wasn't as green here as down by the river. Jessie felt a little strange, as though she was in unfamiliar territory where she didn't belong.

The sheep were grazing quietly along the fence and Jessie walked Magic up behind. The sheep began to move back where she wanted them to go, but then at the last minute they turned away. Jessie slumped in her saddle. This was going to be impossible. What should she do?

She tried once more to guide the sheep back up the track, but again they refused to do what she wanted.

The sun was high overhead and Jessie was getting very hot. It was probably lunchtime, so she decided that the best thing to do was to get help. Jessie imagined Dad would be home from the shops by now and might even be upset with her, but she had to take the chance. It was better than staying out all day trying to round up six sheep and only driving them further and further away.

Magic was tired too, so Jessie sadly turned and guided him home.

When Jessie walked inside the house, hot and streaked with dirt, Mum and Dad didn't look too happy.

'Where have you been?' asked Mum. 'I've being looking all over the place for you.'

'And I was just coming to search for you,' growled Dad.

Jessie hung her head. 'I'm sorry,' she said. 'I've moved the sheep.'

Dad looked confused. 'You've done what?'

'I moved the sheep into the top paddock,' Jessie explained.

Mum scratched her head. 'On your own?'

Jessie nodded. 'Magic and I did it together,' she said.

'All the sheep?' asked Dad, still not believing his ears.

'Well, that's the problem,' admitted Jessie. 'All except for six.'

Dad found it hard to hide his grin. 'Hmmm,' he murmured. 'So where are the six?'

Jessie burst into tears. 'They escaped down the track!'

'Down the track, eh?' Dad said, nodding. 'Hmmm. That's happened to me before. Just a few silly stragglers, off down the track. Useless animals.'

Jessie looked up. 'That's what I think,' she sniffed.

'Right then,' said Dad. 'Let's have lunch. Then you and I will go and round up those stragglers. Did you shut the gates, Jess?'

'Yes,' nodded Jessie.

Mum gave Jessie a hug. 'Please don't disappear again, Jessie. I know you were trying to help, but next time tell us your plans first. Remember the rules?'

Jessie nodded and put her arms around Mum. All of a sudden she felt very tired.

'How's the baby?' she murmured, remembering the big news.

'Fine now,' said Mum. 'A little too much excitement for one baby in one day though. No more adventures today, please, Jessie!'

As they sat down to lunch, Jessie felt better. 'You know,' she said. 'I don't think Magic liked the sheep. But he still worked really hard.'

'So did you,' said Dad. 'We'll take it easy this afternoon. We'll go on the motorbike.'

Jessie grinned. Rounding up sheep on the motorbike with Dad sounded like another great adventure. She sneaked a glance at Mum, but Mum didn't seem to mind at all!

Bush Picnic

It was midnight in the Riverland. Tall trees swayed gently in the moonlight as the breeze tickled their leaves. Inside the old farmhouse at Big Bend Station, everyone was fast asleep in bed. Seven-year-old Jessie Brock was snuggled under her warm quilt dreaming of adventures with her special pony, Magic. Suddenly, she woke up.

A brilliant idea had popped into her head. It was such a great idea that she decided to slip out of bed and peep out of the window. Everything was dark, but Jessie saw a starry sky and a big round moon. There were no clouds. It was just the sort of weather for a picnic!

Jessie jumped back into bed and lay there thinking about where she and

ride to that day. She must
to sleep because when she
the dawn light was
ugh the window. Jessie said
morning' to all the horses and
ponies on her bedroom wall and tiptoed
into her parents' room.

Mum was still asleep but Dad wasn't
there. He often got up early to feed the
animals and do other jobs around the
farm. Jessie crawled into bed with Mum.
She looked at Mum's big tummy and
thought about putting her hand on it to
feel the baby inside moving. But Mum
hadn't been feeling too well lately and
Jessie didn't want to wake her.

Jessie lay still for a minute or two,
planning her picnic lunch. Her backpack
wasn't very big — there was just enough

room for a packet of crisps, an apple, a blueberry muffin, a drink and a carrot for Magic. Jessie knew her Mum would insist she had a sandwich as well, so she would just have to squeeze it in somewhere!

In another pocket of the backpack she'd take her old, brass compass. It had belonged to her grandfather, and Jessie treasured it. Dad had shown her how to use it so she could always find her way home.

While Jessie ate breakfast, Mum prepared the picnic lunch. It was just as Jessie had thought; Mum insisted on the sandwich. Jessie chose the filling: peanut butter, cucumber, carrot, beetroot and mayonnaise. She really hated boring sandwiches!

'Where are you off to today, Jessie?'

asked Mum. 'It must be somewhere good because I can see a twinkle in your eye ... and you can't keep still!'

It was true. Jessie was bouncing up and down.

'Well, Mum, Magic and I are going on a bush picnic,' she explained. 'And we are going somewhere very special! To Big White!

Big White was a huge white sand dune. It was near the big bend in the river where sand had built up over thousands of years. Smaller sand dunes rippled and curved along the riverbank and, then, right in the middle of them all, Big White stood up like a beautiful mountain. It was really a hill but it seemed like a mountain to Jessie. Native bushes and grasses grew all over the sand dunes, holding them together and providing homes for all sorts of birds and insects, spiders and lizards.

Mum was impressed with Jessie's plan. 'How lovely!' she exclaimed. 'I wish I could come with you, but I have to work.'

'Never mind, Mum,' smiled Jessie. 'You can come another time.'

'Okay, I will,' agreed Mum. 'And remember, stay on the tracks!'

Jessie always stayed on the tracks. She had already been lost once in the bush. Anyway, the bush was full of obstacles like branches and bushes and it was too prickly to try to go through them. She hoisted the pack on her back, kissed Mum goodbye and set off for Magic's stable.

Magic was already waiting for her, flicking his black tail impatiently. He looked as handsome as ever. Jessie had washed and brushed him the night before, so his creamy buckskin coat and his black mane and tail gleamed. Jessie's Dad was in the stable too — he must have known Jessie would be going for a ride today. Jessie ran up and gave Dad a hug.

'How did you guess?' she asked.

Dad grinned and tousled her hair. 'It's Saturday isn't it, Jess? No school today. And no prizes for guessing you're going somewhere with Magic this morning!'

Jessie threw the saddle rug across Magic's back and Dad lifted the saddle into place. They buckled the girth, stretched out Magic's forelegs, checked his hoofs for stones, fitted the bridle and adjusted the reins. Soon Magic was ready.

'So, Jess,' said Dad. 'Where are you off to?'

'Magic and I are going to Big White. We're having a bush picnic!'

Jessie was pleased with herself. She had planned the day well.

'Fine,' nodded Dad. 'Just stay on the tracks.'

Jessie looked at him strangely and put her hands on her hips. 'Dad! That's exactly what Mum said!'

'Ahhh, you see, Jess, great minds think alike. We don't want you getting lost.'

'I won't get lost, Dad. I hate getting lost. Anyway, you can't get lost going to Big White. We've been there a hundred times before!'

'That's true,' said Dad. 'Well, don't fall in a prickly bush again!'

Jessie crinkled up her face. She had fallen in a prickly bush once when Magic had wandered away in the bush!

Dad hoisted Jessie up into the saddle and she tested the stirrups. Everything felt fine as usual. Magic was so easy to ride. She nudged him with her heels and off they walked through the gate.

The sun warmed the air and brightened all the colours of the bush. Jessie loved the colours of the outback — the blue-grey-greens of the native plants, trees and shrubs and everything in between. The wildflowers were out too. Lots of small pink, red, blue and yellow flowers were springing up everywhere. Jessie took a deep breath. The scent in the air made her feel very happy.

Magic and Jessie walked along the track, listening to the bush birds calling in the distance. Now and again Jessie nudged Magic into a trot. And when the track was long and straight, Jessie and

Magic cantered happily. Jessie was learning to be a good rider and Magic knew just what Jessie wanted him to do.

Before long they reached the sand dunes near the big bend in the river. Big White looked even bigger and whiter than Jessie could remember. It was covered in little bushes and grasses where lots of tiny creatures lived. There were tracks everywhere, showing where lizards had crawled and small birds had wandered that morning. Fine glistening spiders' webs stretched between the bushes. There was a kangaroo track leading around the base of the sand dune, and diggings where an echidna had foraged during the night.

'Hey, Magic! Isn't this just the best place in the world?' said Jessie. Magic snorted and flicked his black tail. Jessie could tell he liked it too. When Nan visited the farm, Mum, Dad, Nan and Jessie sometimes went to Big White for picnics. There was an excellent swing there too, hanging from the branch of a great old red tree.

Jessie guided Magic carefully between the bushes until they came to the big red gum. She slipped out of the saddle and led her pony to an old fence post with a rope attached. She tied the reins loosely to the rope so Magic had plenty of room to move about and could chew on grass.

Jessie sat on the swing and pushed herself higher and higher until she was swinging way up in the sky each time.

'Magic, look at me!' she squealed. 'I can see everything from up here!' Each time she swung down her tummy felt left behind and she let out a long 'Oooooooooooo.' Each time she swung high Jessie had a great view of the river flowing by on the other side of the dune.

The river was very big and wide, and her parents had always warned Jessie never to swim in it alone or without a life jacket. It could be very dangerous because there were lots of snags under the surface, and boats zoomed up and down it. Pelicans and kingfishers, and ducks and herons flew and swooped above the water or drifted lazily with the current.

Swinging was hungry work and after 43 very high swings, Jessie decided it was picnic time. She unpacked her backpack and fed Magic his carrot. Then she sat down cross-legged under the red tree to eat her sandwich, apple, muffin and crisps.

'Now, Magic, I'm going to climb to the top of Big White. You stay here and watch me, okay?' Magic snorted suddenly, and Jessie laughed. He had stuck his nose into a bush that was covered in tiny white flowers and they had made him sneeze.

Climbing tall sand hills can be hard work, especially when your feet sink deep into the sand with every step. When Jessie finally reached the top of Big White, her legs were tired. She flopped down and buried her hands in the sand. It was cool and smooth on her hot skin. Jessie looked

all around her. Because the sand dune was right near the big bend in the river, she could see the water glistening way into the distance. She lay back and looked up at the sky.

'This sand is really comfy,' she said to herself. 'I could lie here and watch the sky go by all day!' A big black crow cawed lazily in the distance and very soon Jessie was asleep.

She woke up with a start when a fly landed on her nose. At the same time she heard a big splash. Jessie jumped up and looked down at the river. A pelican that had been floating on the river flapped its wings heavily and took off. There was a lot of swirling in the water and Jessie peered closely to see what it was. Her hand flew to her mouth. It couldn't be …

but it was! It was Magic. He was in the river!

Jessie's skin tingled and her heart beat fast inside her chest.

'Magic!' she screamed. 'Magic, what are you doing?'

She tumbled down the dune, avoiding all the bushes and taking huge leaps. Her head was full of questions. Why was Magic in the river? Could he swim? What if the snags got him? What if a boat came along?

Jessie had never been a really fast runner but today she almost flew. When she reached the edge of the river, she saw a little sandy beach with hoof prints.

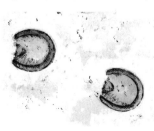

She stopped right on the edge of the water and yelled at the top of her voice, 'MAGIC! COME BACK HERE!'

Jessie could just see Magic's head and he didn't look worried at all. He was swimming happily in crazy circles not far from the river's edge.

Jessie was breathless from shouting. 'Magic ... come here ... at once!' she puffed. 'It's dangerous in the river ... there's snags ... and floating logs ... and boats ... and the current might take you away!'

She was almost in tears. She took one step into the water. 'Magic! PLEASE, Magic!'

Finally, Magic turned his head and began to swim towards her. Jessie stepped back out of the water.

'That's right Magic, come on, come here ...'

At last Magic's hoofs touched the riverbank and he hauled himself out of the water, dripping all over the ground. The saddle was saturated too. Jessie grabbed the soaking reins and pulled him up the bank and away from the water's edge.

Jessie tried to fling her arms around his neck but Magic just wanted to shake the water from his coat and mane. Soon, Jessie was almost as wet as her pony.

'You naughty pony,' she said. 'Where did you learn to swim? You never told me you could swim!' Magic stomped his hoofs and flicked his tail. More water sprayed everywhere.

'The Murray River isn't safe for swimming!' said Jessie. 'You can't just go off like that, Magic.' Magic didn't seem worried although he hung his head, a little tired. Jessie stroked his neck gently. She couldn't be too cross with him.

'You are too adventurous for your own good, Magic,' Jessie said as she rubbed him down with her hands. 'That's what my Mum says to me, and I guess you are just the same.'

Jessie took the reins and walked Magic around for a while. He needed a chance to dry out. Then she looked at her compass to double-check the quickest way home.

At that moment Magic's ears pricked up and Jessie heard the crunching of twigs. She peered along the riverbank and there was Dad riding towards them on his bay mare, Jezebel. Jezebel was a big strong horse and Magic looked tiny next to her.

'Hi, Jessie,' Dad called out. 'How's the picnic?'

'Dad!' exclaimed Jessie. 'You won't believe it! Magic just had a swim in the river and he's soaking wet.'

Dad was surprised. 'You mean he went swimming all on his own?'

'Yes! I was on top of Big White and next thing I knew Magic was in the river!'

Dad jumped off his horse. Jessie threw her arms around him and burst into tears.

'I was so frightened!' she sniffed. 'I thought the snags might get him.'

Dad shook his head. 'You two always get up to mischief!'

'Can we go home now, Dad? I'm soaking wet, and so is Magic.'

'I guess I'm too late for the picnic then,' Dad grinned as he wiped Jessie's damp hair away from her eyes. 'And I was looking forward to a nice cup of billy tea. Oh well, never mind.'

Dad hoisted Jessie into her wet saddle and off they went. Jessie and Magic followed Dad and Jezebel home along the track. Jessie's bottom was soon very wet from the saddle but she didn't really mind. The day had turned out to be more eventful than she had imagined. And Jessie had discovered a very important thing — Magic loved swimming. She'd certainly have to watch him from now on.

A Magic
Mixture

Every morning on Big Bend Station, Dad woke up early to feed all the horses on the farm. Mum's horse was called Starlight and he was a tall, black horse with a gentle nature. Dad's horse was Jezebel and she was a beautiful bay mare, part Clydesdale and very strong. Jessie had named her buckskin pony Magic. He was very special.

There were two other horses on the farm that Dad was breaking in for their owners. Breaking in horses was one of Dad's many jobs. He tamed the young horses and trained them so they could be ridden safely. He did this in between looking after the sheep, running the fruit orchard, keeping chickens and all the other things that farmers do.

Early one summer morning Jessie heard Dad pulling on his boots, so she jumped out of bed and ran into his room.

'Dad, can I come with you today?' she whispered so Mum didn't wake up.

'Sure, Jess,' he whispered back. 'I'll make a cup of tea and then we'll go.'

Jessie pulled on her clothes, gulped down the cup of tea Dad had made for her, and off they went.

Outside, dawn was breaking quietly. The light was still faint with a splash of pink in the sky where the sun would soon appear over the horizon. The birds warbled to each other. Fish made ripples on the river as they plip-plopped their shiny bodies across the surface. A kookaburra began to laugh his incredible laugh, but Jessie knew he wasn't really laughing — he was calling for his mate.

In the hayshed Jessie and Dad loaded bales of hay onto the back of the pick-up. They didn't talk — they both enjoyed the early morning quiet. Then they jumped into the cabin, pulled shut the creaking doors and drove down to the horse paddocks.

All the horses were waiting at the fence for their feed. When Dad and Jessie reached the first paddock they stopped, jumped out and climbed onto the back of the pick-up, which was piled high with hay bales. Together they picked up a hay bale and threw it into the paddock. Then Dad jumped back into the cabin and drove very slowly to the next paddock while Jessie sat happily on the hay bales on the back of the pick-up.

Each time they came to a paddock Dad joined Jessie on the back of the pick-up and they tossed a hay bale over the fence. When they reached the end of the track, Dad turned the pick-up around and they

headed back the way they had come. This time they checked all the troughs for water. Some of the horse troughs were old baths from people's houses. Each had a water pipe leading into it and a float on top to keep the water level constant. Jessie felt very happy helping Dad with the horses, and Dad liked the company.

'Thanks, Jess,' said Dad. 'This is great. It's much quicker when you help.'

When they had checked the last trough they headed back towards Magic's stable. Jessie had ridden Magic around the paddock for hours the day before, so Dad and Jessie had put him in the stable to rest overnight.

'Can I steer the last bit, Dad?' Jessie asked hopefully.

'Sure, Jess, hop onto my lap and take us to Magic's stable.'

Jessie loved sitting on Dad's lap and steering the pick-up along the track. They idled along slowly.

When they reached Magic's stable, Dad stopped the pick-up and Jessie jumped out.

While Dad got Magic some hay, Jessie went into the stable to give Magic a hug. But Magic just stood there, hanging his head. He wasn't interested in his food and he didn't flick his tail when he saw her. Immediately, Jessie knew something was wrong.

She rubbed her hand over his neck and foreleg. He was hot and damp.

'Dad!' she called. 'Come here, quick!'

She looked into her pony's eyes and they were dull, not sparkling as usual.

Dad took one look at Magic. 'He's sick, Jess.' Jessie felt herself go cold. Magic had never been sick before.

'What's wrong with him, Dad?' she squeaked. Dad shook his head. He seemed puzzled.

'I don't know,' he said. 'He was fine last night.'

'He was happy when I rode him in the paddock yesterday,' added Jessie.

Dad picked a few bits of straw from Magic's back. 'He might have a stomach ache. See this straw? It looks like he's been rolling on the ground, something horses often do if their tummies hurt. I'll just check out the paddocks for anything unusual. Back in a minute.'

Jessie stayed with Magic, talking to him softly. Magic nudged his head into her arms and left it there. Jessie put both arms around his neck and hugged him.

'What's up, Magic?' she asked. 'What's wrong? Are you sick?'

She felt him tremble a little in her arms and she was afraid. She just closed her eyes and wished as hard as she could that he would be all right.

When Dad came back, he looked grim.

'How is he, Jess?'

'He's shivering, Dad. What's wrong with him?'

'Hmmm. I found some noxious weed in one of the paddocks.'

Jessie frowned. 'What does "noxious" mean?'

'In this case it means poisonous. I've never seen the weed in our horse paddocks before, but it can spread quickly.'

Jessie's heart missed a beat. 'Is Magic poisoned?'

Dad shook his head. 'I don't know for sure, but the weed could make him sick if he ate any. It's not good for horses.'

Jessie leaned in close to Magic. 'Did you eat any poison weed, Magic?'

Magic didn't move.

Dad cleaned out Magic's stall and gave him lots of clean straw. He even tempted Magic with some special oats, but Magic turned his head away. He wouldn't eat.

Dad made a decision. 'Okay, we'll have to nurse him. You stay here and I'll get Mum. Doug the vet is away at the moment, but Mum knows as much as anyone about sick horses.'

'Please don't be too long,' pleaded Jessie.

While Dad was gone Magic barely moved, except to snuggle his head into Jessie's arms. Her arms were getting tired but she didn't mind. She'd stay like that with him all day and night if she had to.

A few minutes later Mum came quietly into the stable. 'Hi, Jessie, what's this about Magic?'

Jessie looked up sadly. 'He'll be all right, won't he, Mum?'

'Let's have a look.' Mum checked Magic's eyes and gums. Then she pressed her fingers against his neck to count his heartbeat. She pinched the skin at the base of Magic's neck and, last of all, pressed her hand against his tummy.

Jessie couldn't wait any longer. 'What is it, Mum? What's wrong with him?'

'Well, his gums are a bit pale, his heart

is beating just a little fast, and I can feel some gurgling in his tummy. But he isn't dehydrated because his skin goes back to normal after I pinch it.'

'But what's wrong with him?' Jessie insisted.

Mum frowned. 'I can't be sure but it could be colic, or he may have eaten a bit of that poison weed after all.'

'Can we give him some medicine then?' asked Jessie hopefully.

Mum shook her head. 'I can give him an injection to take away the pain, but we'll just have to wait and see how he handles it.'

Jessie's heart seemed to come up into her throat. She was so scared she couldn't even swallow.

'Pity Doug's away for a couple of days. Just when we need him!'

Mum watched Jessie bury her head against Magic's neck. She knew that if Magic had eaten the poison weed he could be seriously ill.

'Jessie,' said Mum, 'I have an idea. I think I can remember the recipe for a special brew that helps sick horses. My mother used to make it years ago for all the sick horses in the district.'

Jessie perked up. 'Can we make it, Mum? Can we make it now? Please?'

Mum agreed. 'Where's Dad? Let's see if he'll keep an eye on Magic for a while.'

Dad was in the paddock with a shovel digging out the poisonous weed when Jessie ran up to him.

'Dad! Can you look after Magic, please?'

Dad straightened his back and wiped his forehead. 'Sure, Jess. How is he now?'

'Mum thinks it might be the poison weed too. Or colic. But she's going to make a special brew for sick horses. And I'm going to help her!'

'Okay, Jess, off you go. I'll keep an eye on Magic.'

'And something else, Dad!'

'What's that, Jess?'

'Magic needs an injection!' Jessie grimaced. 'It won't hurt him, will it?'

Dad shook his head. 'Don't worry, he won't feel a thing.'

Jessie raced back to the stables and gave Magic a big hug and whispered, 'I'll be back soon. And I'll bring some special medicine. You have to get better soon, all right? You just have to!'

She looked into his eyes again, hoping there would be just the hint of a twinkle.

But there wasn't.

Jessie turned and ran as fast as she could after Mum.

In the kitchen Jessie and Mum concocted a strange mixture. It reminded Jessie of making a cake, but it certainly didn't smell like a cake. It had barley meal (a special kind of flour), water and some black drops from a bottle Mum had found at the back of the medicine cupboard.

Jessie stood on a chair and watched as Mum stirred the pot on the stove until it boiled. Then she had to turn down the heat and let it bubble gently for

15 minutes. While this was happening, Mum found all the things she needed for Magic's injection. She wrapped them all in a clean towel and put them in a plastic bag.

'How do you know about sick horses, Mum?'

'When I was little, my parents had lots of horses. And my Mum was a vet, so I learned a few things.'

'Well, I hope our magic mixture works!'

Mum put her arm around Jessie's shoulders. 'So do I, Jessie.'

When the brew was done, Mum added some cold water to cool it down and make it easier to swallow.

'Let's go, Mum.' Jessie was itching to get back to Magic in the stable.

Carrying the brew in a bowl, Jessie burst in through the stable door. Magic was standing just where she had left him.

'Hi, Magic!' Jessie tried to be bright and cheerful. 'Feeling any better?' Magic hung his head listlessly.

'Well, I have something special for you,' said Jessie. 'And you have to eat it. It's a kind of medicine but much nicer! You'll love it, and it'll make you strong.'

Dad came in just as Mum arrived, and while they sorted out the injection, Jessie talked softly to her pony. She held the bowl up to Magic's mouth. 'You'll need lots of energy for all the great adventures we're going to have,' she said. But Magic wouldn't eat the special brew.

Jessie dipped her fingers in the bowl and forced them into Magic's mouth. He

moved his head away but Jessie kept her hand there.

Then, all of a sudden she felt his tongue lick her fingers. Jessie could have danced with happiness.

'Come on, Magic, that's right! Just lick it, and you'll feel heaps better. I know you will!'

Jessie was concentrating so much she didn't even realise that Mum had given Magic his injection. She fed almost the whole bowlful to her pony by dipping her fingers in the mixture and coaxing him to lick it. It took ages, but Jessie didn't notice the time. When she had finished, she hugged Magic gently.

Jessie stayed close to Magic for the rest of the day. For a while she sat in the straw chatting about anything that came into her head. Then she swung upside down on the rail just outside the stable. Later, as the sun was setting and the sky burned orange and red over the river, Jessie sat on a chair and read Magic stories from a book.

Jessie was so absorbed that she didn't hear Dad coming into the stable.

'Time to get ready for bed now, Jess.'

Jessie turned to him pleading, 'Can I sleep here tonight? Magic shouldn't be alone. Please, Dad?'

Dad looked thoughtful. 'I don't know, Jess. I'm not sure it's a good idea.'

'Please, Dad? It *is* a good idea! I can't leave Magic like this. He needs me!'

Dad looked around the stable doubtfully. It was an old wooden building without proper windows.

'Okay, Jess,' he said. 'Tell you what. We'll both sleep here. I'll find a couple of mattresses and you get the sleeping bags. We'll camp out. But just this once.'

Jessie was overjoyed. She tore across the yard to the house and burst in to where her Mum was reading.

'Mum!' she said. 'I'm sleeping with Magic. He needs me.' Jessie explained everything and together they found the sleeping bags.

A little while later, after Mum had persuaded Jessie to eat some dinner, Jessie and Dad were snuggled in their sleeping bags on the mattresses. Jessie was close to her pony. The light from the house shone through the stable door and Jessie could see Magic standing there beside her. He had hardly moved all day, as though he

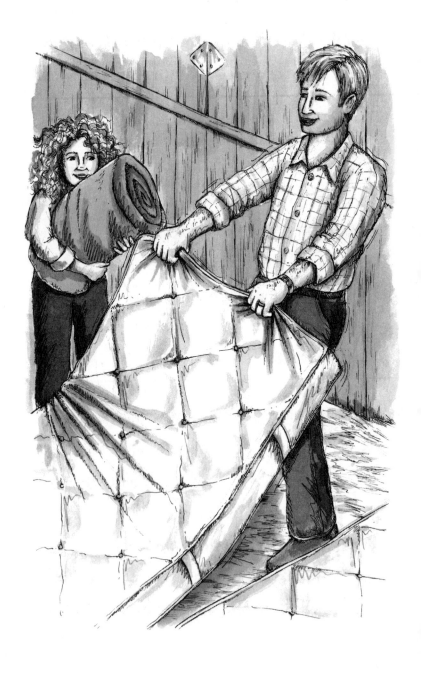

was in a faraway dream. In the dim light Jessie thought how beautiful he looked, with his creamy coat and black mane and tail. She just wished his eyes would sparkle once again.

It had been a long and difficult day and, as much as Jessie tried to stay awake, before long she was fast asleep.

Jessie slept deeply all night. As sunlight streamed in through the stable door the next morning, she heard a familiar sound. There was warm breath on her face and Jessie opened her eyes to see Magic's nose hovering above her own. She squealed in delight and jumped up. As she ran her hand across Magic's back, he raised his head and snorted.

'You're better!' cried Jessie. 'I can tell!' She looked into his eyes and saw just

what she wanted to see — a bit of the Magic sparkle. Jessie was so happy that she jumped and danced around.

Dad heard all the noise and came into the stable. He'd already been out working.

'Dad! He's better!'

'That is excellent news, Jess,' smiled Dad. 'He does seem better, I agree. But take it easy. He must stay quiet today to make sure he gets back to being 100 percent.'

Jessie jumped into her Dad's arms and gave him a big hug.

'It must have been Mum's special medicine,' she said.

'Sure,' agreed Dad. 'And your tender loving care.'

Jessie felt so happy she didn't know what to do, so she did a cartwheel in the straw and danced across the yard to tell Mum the good news.

Magic Goes
to School

The South Australian Riverland was a delicious place to live. Some farms grew oranges, lemons and apricots, while other farms had sheep, cattle and horses. There were almonds and other kinds of nuts, chickens and turkeys, potatoes, carrots and cauliflower. Several farms grew olives for olive oil and even more grew grapes for making wine.

On Jessie's farm there were horses, sheep and chickens, as well as oranges, lemons, apricots and nuts. But Jessie's favourite thing on the farm was Magic, her beautiful buckskin pony. Magic had been a surprise from her parents for her seventh birthday. He had the creamiest coat and blackest mane and tail, and Jessie rode him almost every day.

Jessie missed Magic when she went to

school. She would often look out of the window and dream about him. Once the teacher asked Jessie to share her dream with the class, so Jessie told them all about the time she and Magic went riding after a big storm, and rescued a baby bird that had lost its parents. The teacher and the class liked the story so much that every week they asked Jessie to tell them about her latest adventure.

One morning, Jessie woke up and got ready for school as usual. It was 'crazy colour day', and everyone had to wear the craziest colours they could find. Jessie rummaged through her drawers. She put on some bright yellow trousers, a purple shirt, pink socks, a blue belt, an orange scarf and red sneakers. When she looked at herself in the mirror, she giggled.

She ran into Mum's room and modelled her outfit, spinning round and round. Mum burst into giggles too.

'That's fantastic, Jessie!' she said. 'You look perfect for crazy colour day!'

Jessie and Mum had a quick breakfast and packed Jessie's lunchbox. Then they hurried out to the car to drive to school.

'Mum!' Jessie cried. 'Look at the tyre!'

The front tyre on the car was completely flat. There was no air in it at all.

'Oh, no!' sighed Mum. 'And the spare tyre is still at the garage getting fixed. We took it in yesterday!'

Jessie screwed up her nose! How was she going to get to school? It was too far to walk — it would take more than an hour! Dad could have taken her in his pick-up but he'd driven to the city for business early that morning. Jessie and her Mum looked at each other hopelessly. Neither could think of any way to solve the problem.

'I think you'll have to miss school today, Jessie,' Mum said at last.

'But, Mum! I can't miss today. It's crazy colour day! It's special!'

'I'm not happy about it either, Jessie, but what can we do?' said Mum.

Out of the blue, Jessie suddenly had a brainwave. It was brilliant!

'Mum! I'll ride Magic to school!'

Mum laughed in surprise. 'Ride Magic? But what would you do with a pony at school all day?'

Jessie was serious. In fact, she was really excited about the idea.

'Mum, all the kids at school love Magic! They can't wait to meet him! In my school, Magic is famous!'

Mum smiled. 'I'm sure you're right, Jessie, but what would poor Magic do all day?'

'I'd tie him up to the fence and at break and lunch time I'd take him for a walk.'

Jessie could see Mum was thinking about it.

'Come on, Mum, I am a really good rider and Magic is a really good horse. We can go the back way through the farm, not along the road. It's a lot shorter the back way and it's a wide track. We've ridden on it lots of times.'

Mum was still uncertain.

'I don't think your teacher would be impressed with having a pony at school,' said Mum.

'But, Mum, she would!' exclaimed Jessie. 'She'd be very impressed! Lots of people take their pets to school.'

Mum shook her head. 'But, Jessie, Magic isn't really a pet. Pets are usually small animals like guinea pigs and rabbits!'

'That's right, Mum, so Magic is even better than a pet! My teacher always says she wants to meet Magic!'

Jessie was so excited she was jumping up and down on the spot.

'You could write a note and ask the teacher to phone you as soon as I get to school. So you know I'm safe.'

Mum still wasn't convinced.

'But, Jessie, you'd have to ride Magic home again after school,' she protested.

'That's okay, Mum! Magic can do it, and so can I. We'll come straight home.'

Mum looked at her watch. It was getting later and later. At last, she made a decision.

'Okay, then,' she agreed. 'Get your riding gear and we'll saddle up. I'll walk with you for part of the way.

Jessie was tickled pink! She was going to ride her pony to school! She threw her arms around Mum and gave her a huge

hug. Then she remembered the baby in Mum's tummy.

'Is it okay for you to walk with us, Mum?' asked Jessie. 'You're having a baby soon!'

Mum smiled. 'Walking is very good for me, Jessie.'

A few minutes later Jessie and Mum set out along the bush track towards the town. Jessie and Magic walked slowly and Mum walked beside them. It was a lovely day and they saw wildlife everywhere. A big eagle circled in the sky, looking for some breakfast to catch. A blue-tongue lizard lazed beside the path and poked out his long blue tongue as they went by. Magic had grown so used to the farm that he didn't even shy at the birds or lizards anymore.

When they were almost halfway to the town, Mum stopped.

'Okay, Jessie, you can go the rest of the way on your own.' She pulled an envelope out of her pocket. 'This is a note for the teacher. I'd like her to phone me when you get to school, please.'

Jessie tucked the note in the pocket of her yellow trousers. Mum kissed her goodbye, and then she set off alone with Magic — riding her pony to school.

Jessie and Magic knew every twist of the track, and Jessie felt very safe with Magic. First they passed a paddock of sheep. The sheep turned their heads and stared.

'Silly sheep,' said Jessie.

Then they came to an old stone cottage where shearers had lived many years ago in the old days. The cottage was in ruins and had no roof. Jessie thought it looked silent and sad.

The next thing along the track was an old wooden buggy from the days before cars were invented. Jessie liked the sound of those days. She could have ridden Magic everywhere!

Soon, Jessie and Magic came to a gate in the fence at the end of the bush track. Jessie slipped down, opened the gate and led Magic through. She climbed up on a fence post and back into the saddle. The school gate was a little further on. Jessie was so excited that she didn't even mind that she was late for school.

When Jessie rode up to the classroom, all the children were already inside. A face peered out of the window, then another, and suddenly the whole classroom was in uproar. Everyone pointed and squealed and jumped on tables and fell off chairs. The teacher was surprised too, but not for long. Life in the country was full of surprises.

The whole class rushed outside to meet Jessie and Magic. Jessie handed her teacher the note, and explained about the flat tyre. The children all tried to pat Magic at the same time until the teacher called them away.

Jessie slipped out of the saddle and tied Magic to the fence underneath a shady tree. The teacher sent a couple of students to fetch him a bucket of water

to drink while she went inside to ring Jessie's mother.

Then she herded the children back inside the classroom, but they were still very excited.

'Good morning, everyone,' she said.

'Good morning, Ms Jolly,' they chanted in reply.

'It's a very good morning today,' said Ms Jolly. 'It's a very colourful morning too.'

She looked around the room and smiled. The children were dressed in every bright colour under the sun. She almost needed sunglasses!

'We also have a special visitor,' she said. 'We've heard a lot about Magic, and today we are very lucky to meet him.'

Ms Jolly smiled at Jessie. 'Jessie, would you like to give us a morning talk about your very latest adventure with Magic?'

As Jessie described her ride to school, the teacher noticed that every few seconds someone looked out of the window to see if Magic was all right. She decided to make some changes to her lessons for the day.

'Thank you, Jessie. That was great. Now, since it is crazy colour day, we'll start with some painting. Let's all go outside and paint a picture.'

The children thought this was a great idea. They quickly put on their artshirts, took their paints and paper outside, and set to work. The teacher walked around looking at all the pictures, and wasn't surprised to find that everyone was painting Magic.

He looked so handsome, with his flashing eyes and his black tail swishing away the flies. Jessie was very proud. All the children were concentrating hard, looking up at Magic and painting their pictures.

At the end of the lesson, there were 20 magnificent paintings of Magic. Ms Jolly decided to make an art gallery in the classroom, and they spent the rest of the morning hanging all the paintings on the walls.

Ellie 7

Mark 7

Ruby 8

Soon it was time for lunch.

Magic couldn't believe his luck. Every child had an apple or carrot, nuts or apricots, or other yummy Riverland goodies that they wanted to share with Magic. The teacher was busy making sure the children didn't give all their lunch away. Jessie was busy making sure Magic didn't eat too much — they still had a long ride home!

By the end of the day, Ms Jolly was exhausted. The children just wanted to look at Jessie's pony. The only way she could get them to concentrate in the maths lesson was to say, 'Now, if we had two ponies, and another two ponies came along, how many ponies would we have?' Or, 'If there were seven ponies in the paddock and four ponies ran away, how many ponies would be left?'

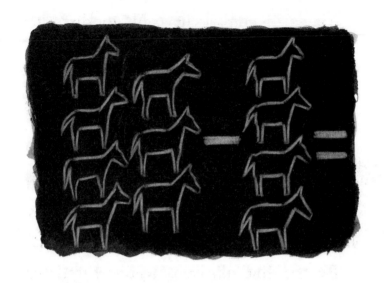

In the spelling lesson the only words the children wanted to spell were words like 'saddle', 'buckle', 'bridle', 'reins', 'stable' and 'veterinary'. And in reading, the children asked for a story about a pony. Since Ms Jolly couldn't find one anywhere, she had to invent one on the spot.

When the home bell rang, the whole class raced outside to say goodbye to Magic. Ms Jolly came out too, and walked up to Magic to pat him.

'Thank you, Magic,' she said, 'for giving us so many interesting things to think about today.' The children all clapped loudly and cheered. It was the best day at school they could remember.

But at that moment, Magic lifted his tail and did something he shouldn't have, right by the teacher's foot. Jessie turned bright red with embarrassment. The children giggled.

Jessie thought she should disappear as quickly as possible. She pulled on her riding hat, scrambled up onto the fence and slipped into the saddle. She waved goodbye, nudged Magic with her boots

and off they went towards the farm. Magic seemed glad to be off too. They soon found their way onto the sandy bush track that would lead them home.

It was a calm afternoon with a slight breeze in the treetops. The bush looked and smelt wonderful, and soon Jessie felt better. Jessie could feel Magic relax too. It must have been very strange for him, she thought, surrounded by all those children at school.

Mum was at the halfway mark, sitting on a log by the track, waiting patiently. Jessie was glad to see her and together they wandered home, Jessie telling Mum the story of Magic's day at school. When she described what Magic did at the end of the day, Mum couldn't stop laughing.

'Never mind, Jessie,' she giggled. 'The

flat tyre is fixed now. You won't have to ride Magic to school again.' Jessie was relieved. It had been a great day, but she wasn't sure she wanted another one just like it.

After dinner, Jessie wrote a letter to the teacher, thanking her for making crazy colour day so much fun. She also apologised for her pony's manners. Then she curled up in bed with Mum and fell fast asleep.

The New
Moon

When Jessie woke up in the middle of the night, it was pitch black. Often some moonlight twinkled into her room past the edge of the curtains, but not tonight. Jessie slipped out of bed and peeked out of her window at the Milky Way. There were no clouds, just thousands of faraway stars. Jessie wondered if anyone had ever counted all the stars in the sky. She looked everywhere for the moon, but it wasn't there. It must be a 'new' moon, Jessie decided. That meant the moon was invisible and helped explain why it was so dark outside.

Jessie remembered stories about amazing things that happened when the moon was full and when the moon was new. Her uncle had told her that fish

were easier to catch on a full moon, and her nana believed that if you planted seeds when the moon was full they grew more quickly. Jessie's nana also said that the new moon was a good time for rest. So Jessie went back to sleep dreaming about the stars and the invisible moon.

As dawn began to creep across the Riverland, Jessie crawled into bed with Mum. Dad had already got up to do some work on the farm so there was plenty of room in the big bed for Jessie. She laid a hand on Mum's round tummy. She could feel the baby stretching inside.

'It feels big, Mum!' whispered Jessie.

'It does,' said Mum, 'but I hope it isn't! You were tiny when you were born, even though my tummy looked enormous! I thought I was going to have a whale!'

Jessie giggled and looked at Mum's tummy again. 'When will our baby be born?' she asked.

'Soon, I think,' smiled Mum. 'Perhaps in a week or two.'

'Not today or tomorrow?' asked Jessie, with a strange feeling in her own tummy.

'I certainly hope not,' said Mum, 'because Dad is very busy on the farm at the moment. I think this baby can wait until next week at least.'

'So do I,' agreed Jessie. 'That would be much better.'

Jessie could see that Mum was tired so she decided to bring her breakfast in bed. She made a cup of tea, a bowl of muesli and a piece of toast with homemade apricot jam. Jessie felt very proud as she carried in the tray and set it down on the

bedside table. Mum was happy too, because she really didn't feel like getting up just yet.

Jessie sat on the edge of the bed and chatted to Mum about her day. She wanted to go for a ride on Magic. She had been at school all week and all she wanted now was some fun with her pony.

'Magic has never seen the baby lambs, so I want to take him for a special ride to see them,' explained Jessie.

'Sounds like a good idea,' agreed Mum. 'Perhaps you could count them for us. I have no idea how many baby lambs we have this year.'

Jessie was excited. She loved doing useful jobs on the farm.

'Okay, Mum, I will. And you should have a good rest while I'm gone,' said

Jessie in a voice that sounded just like her Mum.

It was a lovely warm day with a clear blue sky, a gentle breeze and plenty of bush scents. Jessie could smell the wildflowers as she walked up to Magic's stable.

Dad was nowhere in sight, so Jessie saddled up. It took a long time all on her own. The bridle was easy but the saddle was heavy to lift. Then she had to buckle the girth and stretch out Magic's forelegs. Her last job was to check his hoofs for stones.

At last, Jessie climbed the rail and

slipped across into the saddle. She took a deep breath.

'Thanks, Magic, I know you tried to help, but it's still hard work!' Jessie patted his neck. 'Anyway, now it's your turn. Let's go!'

With a big smile, Jessie patted Magic and they set off up the track.

Jessie counted 17 baby lambs in the lambing paddock. She loved to watch them; they were small and white with wobbly legs. Most of them stayed as close to their mothers' bellies as they could.

Jessie was about to turn back when she saw that one of the tiny lambs seemed to be lost. It was bleating pitifully, and its little legs were especially wobbly. There was a sheep grazing nearby without a lamb at all, and Jessie wondered if it was the mother.

Jessie slipped her feet out of the stirrups and slid off Magic's back onto the ground.

'You stay there, Magic,' she whispered.

Jessie walked slowly up to the baby lamb. It looked at her with frightened eyes and bleated again.

She reached her arms around the baby lamb and picked it up. It was heavy, but she couldn't bear it to be lost. She staggered her way over to the lone sheep, and put the lamb down beside it. The sheep didn't move away, and to Jessie's delight the lamb quickly found its way under the sheep for a drink of milk.

'Now you look after your baby, you silly sheep!' she scolded. The mother sheep just blinked at her.

Feeling very pleased with herself, Jessie led Magic to the fence and climbed back into the saddle. She played with Magic's

black mane as she sat in the saddle and watched the lamb drink happily from its mother.

'Lambs are cute, aren't they, Magic?' she said. 'But they're not beautiful like you. You are the best!'

Jessie thought she'd better wash her hands after picking up the lamb, so she decided to go home. She turned Magic around and they cantered back along the track towards the house, the breeze in their faces.

Jessie tied Magic's reins to the garden fence near the farmhouse. She pulled off her riding boots and skipped inside.

'Hi, Mum!' Jessie called as she went into the bathroom and ran the tap to wash her hands. 'I just saved a baby lamb!'

There was no answer. Jessie dried her hands on a towel, and then looked in the bedroom. The bed was empty. She looked in the kitchen and that was empty too. She looked out into the back garden, but Mum wasn't anywhere.

Then she heard her name being called softly. Jessie was puzzled.

'Mum? Where are you?'

'In here,' called Mum, quietly.

Jessie peeped into her own bedroom and found Mum sitting on the bed with a pained look on her face.

'Mum, what's wrong?' cried Jessie.

'It's all right, darling. Everything's fine. I was just cleaning up, but then I had a funny feeling and I think I'm going to have the baby very soon. Can you go and find Dad for me?'

'Sure!' said Jessie. 'Do you need anything?' Jessie was concerned.

'No, Jessie, I'll be okay.'

'You just stay here, Mum. I'll get help.'

Jessie sped out of the house, threw on her boots, climbed the fence and jumped onto Magic's back. She took up the reins and urged Magic into a canter. When they reached the paddocks on top of the hill, Jessie brought Magic to a halt. She looked around. Where was Dad? Jessie thought he would be up here with the sheep but she couldn't see him. Where should she look next? Jessie tried to remember where he said he would be today. Was he down in the fruit block or mending the broken fence ... or was he building the new hay shed?

Jessie took a guess and tried the fruit

block. She and Magic rode in and around rows of orange trees but couldn't see anyone at all. Jessie turned back and rode to the hay shed, but again there was no one around. She was getting worried. Mum was at home waiting for help to have her baby, and Jessie couldn't find Dad anywhere. Perhaps he had driven over to the next station or taken a load of hay somewhere.

She had one last idea. Jessie knew that the fence along the road was broken and Dad had been trying to find time to fix it before the baby was born. It was a long ride, halfway to town, but Jessie didn't mind. She turned Magic back up the track and set off for the main road. When they reached the fence, Jessie turned to follow the track inside the fence. She peered into the distance, searching for signs of Dad and his pick-up.

At last she came to the broken part of the fence, but Dad wasn't there. Jessie's heart skipped a beat. Where could he be? She had looked everywhere!

All of a sudden Jessie knew what she had to do. She took a deep breath and leaned down to rub Magic on the neck.

'Magic,' she whispered urgently, 'I can't find Dad so we have to ride into town to get the doctor. It's not very far because we're halfway there already. But we have to go fast. Can you do it? Can you help me, my beautiful pony?'

Magic tossed his head in the air, snorted and flicked his black tail. He couldn't wait to get going again.

'Okay then, Magic, let's go!'

Jessie nudged him into a canter and they set off towards the town.

The track was flat and sandy, and they seemed to fly along it. Jessie kept a lookout for animals and obstacles in the way. She couldn't fall off now! They had to reach the doctor as soon as they could.

She and Magic were lucky. It was a lovely sunny day and the track was clear and easy to ride. A few cockatoos screeched overhead as they flew off their branches in the trees, but Magic was used to Riverland birds now.

It was tiring work, and both Jessie and Magic were perspiring with the effort.

Jessie wondered if Magic would be able to keep going, but he seemed to know how important it was and he didn't slow down.

At last they came to the farm boundary, and Jessie had to dismount and open the gate. Magic waited for her to stand on the fence, climb back in the saddle and off they went again, up the road to the doctor's surgery. Jessie could see cars there so she knew the doctor was in. She rode right up to the door, slipped off her pony once again, threw the reins over a post and ran inside.

The patients in the waiting room were very surprised when a dishevelled seven-year-old girl in a riding hat burst in and asked for the doctor. The nurse looked at Jessie in amazement.

'Mum's having a baby and I can't find Dad anywhere,' gasped Jessie. 'She needs the doctor at once!'

'Is your mother having the baby now?' asked the nurse. 'Right now?'

'I think so!' nodded Jessie. 'And she's all alone.'

'I see!' said the nurse. 'Then I'll get the doctor straight away.'

The nurse disappeared through a door, but in a few seconds she came back and explained to the waiting patients that an emergency had come up. She asked them to please come back later. Then the doctor hurried out of the surgery and got into his car.

All of a sudden Jessie felt dizzy and had to sit down on a chair. The nurse brought her a glass of water.

'I'm going over to see your Mum now too,' said the nurse. 'Would you like a lift home?'

Jessie shook her head. 'No, thanks, I came here on my pony so I'll have to ride him home. But can I have a bucket of water to give him a drink first, please?'

Magic was waiting patiently outside the doctor's surgery. He was very thirsty and slurped up the water Jessie had brought him. As the nurse left in her car, Jessie flung her arms around Magic's neck.

'Thank you, Magic,' she whispered. 'Thanks for bringing me here. I know Mum and our baby will be safe now.'

Jessie just wanted to be back home with Mum and make sure she was all right. She knew the doctor would be there by now, and hopefully Dad had got there too. So Jessie climbed into the saddle, and off they went.

The afternoon sun was setting as Jessie and Magic walked wearily into the home paddock. Jessie had wanted to canter some of the way but she knew Magic couldn't go any faster.

Jessie made sure that Magic had plenty of water and left him in the paddock. She was too tired to unsaddle him and put everything away. When at last she reached the front door of the house, Jessie's legs were so wobbly she could hardly walk. But when she opened the door, she couldn't believe her eyes.

Mum was sitting in her armchair, smiling, and holding the tiniest baby in her arms. The doctor and the nurse were sitting there too, having a cup of tea.

With tears in her eyes, Jessie ran over to Mum and hugged her. Mum hugged her back.

'My darling, Jessie,' she said. 'You are the cleverest, most wonderful daughter. The doctor arrived just in time, and all because of you and Magic. This is your beautiful baby brother.'

Jessie looked at the baby in Mum's arms. He was her new brother and he was perfect. 'One baby brother and 17 baby lambs!' said Jessie. 'Wow!' Everyone laughed.

'Where's Dad?' she said, suddenly.

The door opened behind her and Dad walked in.

'Jessie, I've been out looking for you!' he exclaimed. Jessie jumped into his arms.

'You are the best, Jess!' said Dad. He gave her a big hug.

Suddenly Jessie burst into tears. But they were tears of happiness because she must surely be the luckiest person in the whole wide world.

Animals in Magic's World

Cockatoo – type of parrot with a crest on its head

Echidna – a toothless burrowing mammal with spines like a hedgehog

Galah – a cockatoo with a rose-coloured chest and grey back

Honey-eater –a bird with a long tongue that can take nectar from flowers

Kookaburra – a kind of kingfisher known for a loud laughing call

Lizard – a reptile with a long body and tail and a scaly hide

Pelican – a waterfowl with a pouch in its beak for storing fish

Puggles – baby echidnas

Skink – a small lizard